Basil Brush finds Treasure

For Emily

PETER FIRMIN

Basil Brush
finds
Treasure

KAYE & WARD
and
SCHOLASTIC PUBLICATIONS

First published by
KAYE & WARD LIMITED
21 New Street, London EC2M 4NT
1971
Reprinted 1975

ISBN 0 7182 0324 0 (hardback)
ISBN 0 7182 0344 5 (paperback)

All enquiries and requests relevant to this title
should be sent to the publisher, Kaye & Ward Ltd,
21 New Street, London EC2M 4NT, and not to
the printer.

Printed in England by
TINLING (1973) LTD

Basil Brush is a happy fox.
His holidays are happy
in his cottage by the sea.

He works in the garden.

He walks in the forest.

He watches the sea-birds on the cliffs.

He plays ball-games with Harry.
Harry is a mole.

Harry likes doing all these things,
but best of all, Harry likes digging.
He digs in the garden.

He digs in the forest.

He digs near the cliffs.
and makes friends with the sea-birds.

One day Basil was very busy.
He was clearing out the summer house.
"I wish you would help me, old chap,"
he said to Harry. "I can find you
a much more useful job than digging."

"But digging is very useful," said Harry.
"I find many useful things. I have already
found a rusty key, a six-inch nail and an
old clay pipe. Who knows, one day I may
even find treasure."

"Ha! ha! yes. One day!" laughed Basil.
"Treasure would be very useful. Now come
and help me in here, there's a good chap."

So Harry and Basil cleared out the summer
house. They found boxes, empty lemonade
bottles and broken deck-chairs.
Not very useful things to find.

"Look," said Harry. "This might be useful.
I have found an old leather bag."
He opened the bag and looked inside.
He saw a pair of goggles, a bucket of sand,
a fishing-line and a teddy-bear.
"They are the things I left behind
last year," said Harry. "I thought
I had lost my teddy-bear."

"What was his name?" asked Basil.

"He never had one," said Harry.

"What!" cried Basil. "A teddy without a name; a nameless bear; how sad! A poor lost nameless teddy-bear. How very sad!"

"I was very fond of him," said Harry.

"But I never could find a name for him. Then I lost him. Shall I call him 'Lost'?"

"No," said Basil. " 'Lost' is not the right name for your bear, because now you have found him. Look after him while I finish clearing out the summer house."

Basil swept the floor while Harry sat
with his teddy-bear.
"Look," said Basil. "Now I have found
something. Here is a trapdoor.
I wonder what is underneath."

Basil lifted the trapdoor.
Underneath was a tunnel.
"That," said Harry, "is a tunnel. I like
tunnels. Moles know all about tunnels."
"I say, old chap," said Basil. "Is it one
of yours? Have you lost a tunnel as well
as a teddy-bear?"
"Oh, no," said Harry. "I never lose tunnels.
It is not one of mine. Do you think I should
call my teddy-bear 'Tunnel'?"

"No," said Basil. " 'Tunnel' is not a
suitable name for your bear."
Basil and Harry went into the tunnel.
Harry took his teddy-bear and
all the other things in the bag.
It was very dark in the tunnel, but Basil
followed Harry, who had very sharp eyes.

Soon they came to the end of the tunnel.
At the end of the tunnel was a cave.
"Look!" said Harry. "Look at that boat.
I wonder whose boat it can be. Perhaps
it is a smuggler's boat. Shall I call my
teddy-bear 'Smuggler'?"

"No," said Basil. " 'Smuggler' is not a
good name for your bear. Look, there is
a 'B' for Basil painted on that boat.

Last year there was a bad storm
in the harbour and my boat was swept away.
That is not a smuggler's boat. That is
my boat. Come on, the oars and the anchor
are still there, and the boat is floating,
let us take the boat out."

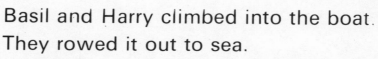

Basil and Harry climbed into the boat.
They rowed it out to sea.
"Shall we anchor the boat and look
for sunken treasure?" said Basil.
"Treasure would be very useful."

"Yes," said Harry. "I will wear my goggles.
I will dive down into the sea
and look for treasure."
Basil dropped the anchor to the bottom
of the sea so that the boat would not
drift away.

Harry jumped into the water.
He swam down to the bottom of the sea.
He saw fish and he saw seaweed
but he did not see any treasure.
He soon bobbed up again.

"You did not stay down long," said Basil.
"It is not very easy to stay under the
water," said Harry. "I need something
heavy to keep me down."

Basil looked in the bag.

"Here's the very thing," he said.

"This bucket of sand is heavy. If you
stand in the bucket I will lower you
down with the fishing-line."

Basil tied the line to the handle
of the bucket and Harry stood inside.
"Pull on the line and I will know
that you want to come up," said Basil.
"And don't forget to hold your breath."

Basil lowered Harry and his bucket
to the bottom of the sea.

Harry looked around him.
He saw fish.
He saw seaweed.
Then he saw a rope.

He hooked the fishing-line to the rope.
He pulled on the line so that Basil
would pull him up.

Basil pulled Harry into the boat.
"Have you found treasure?" he said.
"I have found some old rope," said Harry.
"Perhaps there is treasure
on the end of it."

Basil pulled on the rope. It was very heavy.
"There is something on the end," he said.

Then they saw what was on the end of
the rope. Harry looked around.
''We seem to be drifting,'' he said.

"Yes, you silly old mole," said Basil.
"Of course we are drifting. We have pulled
up our own anchor."

"Oh dear," said Harry. "How silly.
Well you'd better throw it back again."
Basil dropped the anchor back into
the water. (Neither Basil nor Harry
noticed that the bag fell in too.)

Basil lowered Harry and his bucket
to the bottom of the sea.

Harry looked around him.
He saw fish.
He saw the anchor.
Then he saw a barrel.

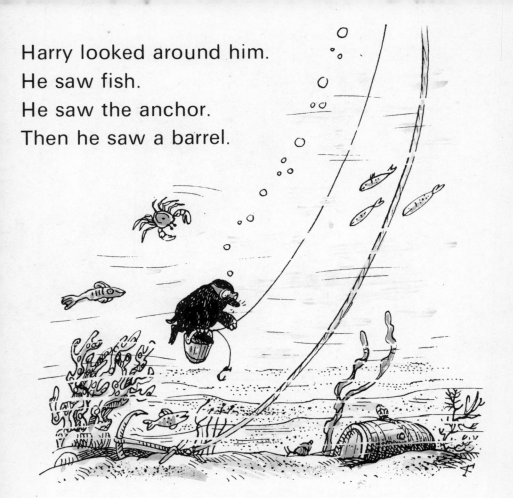

He hooked the fishing-line to the barrel.
He pulled on the line so that Basil would
pull him up.

Basil pulled Harry into the boat.
"Well, have you found treasure?" he asked.
"I have found a barrel," said Harry.
"Perhaps it's full of gold coins."

Basil lifted the barrel into the boat.
He pulled out the cork.
It was not full of gold coins.
It was full of salt water.

They threw it back.
"What a pity," said Harry. "It was such
a promising barrel. Shall I call my
teddy-bear 'Barrel'?"
"No," said Basil. " 'Barrel' is not a kind
name for your bear. Will you try again?"

Basil lowered Harry and his bucket
to the bottom of the sea.
Harry looked around him.
He saw fish.
He saw the anchor.
He saw the barrel.

Then he saw a bag, lying in the sand
among the seaweed.
"Surely this must be treasure," he thought.

He hooked the fishing-line to the bag.
He pulled on the line and Basil pulled him up.
"I've done it! I have! This time I really
have found treasure," gasped Harry. "It's
a bag and there is something inside it."

"Oh, you little wet wonder!" said Basil.
"Have you really? Let's see."
Basil pulled the bag into the boat.
He opened it and looked inside.

"Oh, Harry," he said. "Guess what you have found this time."

"Is it gold?" asked Harry.

"No, old chap," said Basil. "Try again."

"Is it silver?" asked Harry.

"Not that either," said Basil.

"Well is it just pennies?" said Harry.

Basil turned the bag upside down.

Something fell out.

It was not gold.

It was not silver.

It was not even just pennies.

It was Harry's teddy-bear!

`Basil laughed: "Ha! ha!"
He roared: "Ho! ho! ho!"
He laughed so much that he could not
stand up: "Haw! haw! he! he! he!"
He fell over backwards into the bottom
of the boat. He stopped laughing.

"Oh, Harry," he said. "I feel all wet.
I think I've made a hole in the boat."
"Shall I help you up?" asked Harry.
"If I get up," said Basil, "the water will
come in and the boat will sink. Give me
something to stuff into the hole."

Harry gave Basil the only thing he had—
the teddy-bear. Basil stuffed the
teddy-bear into the hole and stood up.
"Harry old friend," he said. "I am wet and
I am tired. I think we have had enough
of the sea for today. Let us go home."

They rowed the boat to the shore.
Harry took the bear out of the boat and
squeezed him until he was nearly dry.
"It has been a good day for finding lost
things," said Basil. "We have found a
lost bag, a lost tunnel and a lost boat.
They were all very useful things to find."

"Yes, and I found my lost teddy-bear,"
said Harry. "He was useful, too.
And I've found a name for him at last.
I shall call him 'Treasure'."
"Yes," said Basil. " 'Treasure' is a very
good name for your bear. I think he is
the most useful thing we have found today."

"Of course he is," said Harry.
"After all, you did say 'Treasure would
be very useful,' didn't you?"

the end